W9-AFX-042

Misty Knows

A novel by

Liz Brown

HIP-JR.

HIP Junior
Copyright © 2006 by High Interest Publishing

All rights reserved. No part of this book may be reproduced or
transmitted in any form or by any means electronic, mechanical,
optical, digital or otherwise, or stored in a retrieval system
without prior written consent of the publisher. In the case of
photocopying or other reprographic reproduction, a licence from
CANCOPY may be obtained.

Library and Archives Canada Cataloguing in Publication

Brown, Liz, 1981–
    Misty knows / Liz Brown.

(HIP jr)
ISBN 1-897039-21-2

I. Title. II. Series.

PS8603.R685M57 2006   jC813'.6   C2006-903373-0

General editor: Paul Kropp
Text design and typesetting: Laura Brady
Illustrator: Izabela Ciesinska
Cover design: Robert Corrigan

    2 3 4 5 6 7   16 15 14 13 12 11

Printed in Canada

High Interest Publishing acknowledges the financial support of
the Government of Canada through the Canada Book Fund for
our publishing activities.

Someone is putting poison in the feed at Mr. Long's stable. Jen and Keisha think they know who's doing it, but first they have to find some proof.

CHAPTER 1

Misty Is in Trouble

The field outside the stable door was fresh with morning dew. The sun was shining bright. There was no hint of trouble. On a day like this, how could there be any trouble?

That's when my best friend Keisha ran out from the barn. "Jen! Have you heard?"

"Heard what?" I asked her. I was cleaning off my saddle and getting ready to ride.

"Mr. Long might sell the farm!"

I sighed. Keisha is cool and smart, but she's

also a gossip queen. I used to get worried when she told me stuff like this. But most of the time Keisha gets the story wrong.

"So where did you hear that?" I asked her.

"On my way over here," Keisha said. "I saw a big red SUV pull into the driveway. I was thinking what a nice car it was when a guy with slicked-back hair and a dark suit climbed out. He knocked on Mr. Long's door."

"So? You've got something against slicked-back hair and suits?" I asked her.

Keisha rolled her eyes. "This isn't just gossip, Jen. I know I've been wrong in the past, but I think this is serious!"

"Okay, okay," I said. "So tell me."

"Anyway, I heard the suit guy start talking to Mr. Long. He said Mr. Long could get a lot of money for the farm, like more than a million dollars!" Keisha's eyes were very wide.

But I wasn't surprised. The city was growing into the country. Lots of farmers had sold already. New houses were going up each day. They call it

a real estate boom. But it means that all the old farms are going, one by one.

"So what did Mr. Long say?"

"He told the guy he wasn't interested. He said something like, 'I told you before, no sale!' Then Mr. Long shut the door on him. But the suit-guy didn't give up. He shouted at Mr. Long, 'You'll change your mind, old man!'"

"It's nothing," I said. "After all, Mr. Long told the guy no. That's that."

But I had to admit, I was a little bit worried. This guy in the suit sounded serious. If Keisha was right, maybe Mr. Long was in some kind of trouble. Maybe the suit-guy could force Mr. Long to sell.

"How can you stay so calm about all this?" Keisha snapped back.

"Because one of us has to be," I told her. "And you're already bouncing off the wall. Come on, let's go riding. We can ask Mr. Long about it at our lesson tomorrow."

Even though we were both a little worried,

it didn't stop us from riding. We headed to the field to catch our two favorite ponies, Misty and Frosty. Misty was "my" pony. Frosty was Keisha's. Even though Mr. Long owned them, it felt like we did. We brushed them and cleaned their stalls all summer. It was a trade-off. We helped with the horses and Mr. Long let us ride them. It was as close as we could get to having our own ponies. Neither of our parents could afford to buy us one.

Even worse, my parents couldn't afford to pay for riding lessons anymore. About a month ago my dad told me I would have to quit. "We don't have the money to keep you in a rich kid's sport like that," he said. I knew my mom was behind it. She was always nervous about me and horses. "What if you fall off and break your neck?" she would ask.

Anyway, I was real upset when they told me. But when I told Mr. Long about it, he told me not to worry. "You just keep taking care of Misty and I'll keep teaching you," he said. "No problem."

That's just the kind of man Mr. Long was. He

didn't run his stable like some of the snobby ones. Most of the kids at Shady Acres didn't have much money. Mr. Long was always giving deals and letting the kids work for their lessons. One day my dad asked Mr. Long how he made any money. I was ready to kill my dad, but Mr. Long just laughed. "I'm an old man," he said. "I've got enough money to keep me and the farm going. That's all I care about."

So we were lucky, Keisha and me. On this bright, early morning we could get out and ride. As we got closer to the gate, I could see Frosty waiting to be brought into the barn. But where was Misty? I climbed up on the fence and looked around the field. "Over there," pointed Keisha.

In the farthest corner of the field I could see Misty. She was lying down.

Right away I knew something was wrong. Misty didn't just lie down like that. She was the kind of pony that had to be the first in the barn. She was always waiting at the gate to come in.

Without thinking, I jumped off the fence and

started running toward her. "Go back and get Mr. Long," I shouted at Keisha. "We need help."

When I got closer, I could see that Misty was breathing hard and sweating. She looked really scared. When I touched her, I could feel her shake.

"Oh, Misty," I whispered. I had to try hard not to cry. I sat down beside her and put her head in my lap. I scratched her ear just where she liked it. *If only Misty could talk*, I said to myself. She must know what's gone wrong. If she could only tell me what happened, maybe I could help her.

"Don't worry girl, you're going to be okay," I told her.

But inside, I was really scared. "Please, Misty," I whispered in her ear, "just hang on."

CHAPTER 2

Maybe I'm Getting Old

Ten minutes later, Mr. Long and Keisha came running into the field.

"Don't worry, Jen," Mr. Long shouted. He was way out of breath. "I've already called the vet. He's on his way!"

I looked down at Misty and ran my hand over her cheek. "Did you hear that, Misty?" I told her. "You just have to hang in there a little longer. We're getting some help."

Misty seemed to look up at me. It was as if

she wanted to say thanks, thanks for getting help. Then she closed her eyes and seemed to sleep.

When Mr. Long got down beside me, he looked worried. "This is worse than I thought," he said. "We need to get this pony up and walking around." "Lying here ain't doin' her no good."

I moved away as Mr. Long put a halter on Misty's head. Then he put on a lead rope. "Okay, girls, grab this rope. When I say pull, you pull as hard you can." Then he walked behind Misty and started pushing on her butt. "Pull," he shouted as he kept pushing. "Harder!"

Keisha and I started pulling as hard as we could. We both knew it was important for Misty to get up. We had to get her to the stable.

"Come on, Misty. I know you can do it," shouted Keisha.

That shout from Keisha seemed to be all that Misty needed. She put her front legs out. Then she used all her strength to pull herself to her feet.

"Good girl," I told her.

At first I was happy that Misty was up. But

when I looked at her, I knew she was very sick. Her head was hanging down low. She was still sweating. And now she was starting to shake again. I stood there for a minute, not knowing what to do.

"I'll take her from here, Jen," said Mr. Long.

I followed Mr. Long and Misty back to the barn. It took everything I had to not burst into tears. At last I saw Doc Vickers, the vet, pull into the driveway. He'd know what to do.

"It'll be okay, now," I told Misty. "Doc Vickers is here. He'll know what to do."

Misty breathed hard. Did she understand? Or did she know what would happen next?

It took forever to get Misty into the barn. At last we got Misty into her stall. Mr. Long went out to talk to Doc Vickers while we held Misty's head.

We could see Doc Vickers look around in the back of his truck. At last he found what he needed. Doc Vickers walked up to the stall with a large needle in his hand.

Misty looked at him, then at me. She was scared — I could tell.

All three of us held on to Misty. Quickly, Doc Vickers stuck the needle in her neck. Misty whinnied from the pain, but soon the shot began to help.

Doc Vickers looked at Mr. Long. "You're lucky you found this pony when you did," he said. "A few more minutes and I don't think she would've made it."

"It was really the girls who found her," Mr. Long replied.

"So is Misty going to be okay?" I broke in. "I mean, *really* okay?"

"She'll be fine," said the vet. "She just needs a little rest in her stall and a lot of care for the next few days. You girls don't mind looking after a sick horse, do you?"

I was so relieved, I wanted to give Doc Vickers a big hug. I could see that Misty was already feeling better. Her breathing had slowed down and she wasn't trembling any more. She was even lifting her head a little.

"So what was wrong with her?" asked Mr. Long.

"I've never had a problem with this pony before."

The vet looked around at all of us. "She must have eaten something that wasn't too good for her," he said.

"You mean like poison?" asked Keisha.

"Oh, Keisha," I said. "Get real."

Doc Vickers just shook his head. "I don't know what she ate," the vet said. "But it was something toxic. It could've been some bad feed, or something in the field . . . who knows?"

Toxic. That means, like, poison. *Maybe Keisha wasn't crazy*, I thought.

"There has to be some kind of mistake," broke in Mr. Long. "There's not one thing in my whole field that could poison a pony."

I had to agree with Mr. Long. He was out all the time checking over that field. Keisha and I had even helped him clear out the plants one spring. And he never used any kind of spray around the farm.

Doc Vickers looked at the three of us. "I know when a horse has eaten something it shouldn't

have," said the vet. "This horse ate something toxic.
Better start thinking what it could have been."

Doc Vickers packed up his stuff and drove off.
That's when I tried to think how Misty could have
gotten sick. I mean, maybe a kid gave her a rotten
apple or carrot. A lot of the kids brought treats for
the ponies. But I didn't think a bad apple or carrot
could make a horse that sick.

Misty knows, I said to myself. Only Misty knows what made her sick, and she can't tell us.

"What do you think she ate?" Keisha asked Mr. Long.

"I really don't know, girls," he replied, patting Misty. My favorite horse was looking even more like her old self again. "I thought I was careful, but maybe I missed a few weeds."

"You couldn't have," said Keisha. "I've helped you pull them out before. We all know how careful you are!"

"Maybe I'm just getting too old," he sighed. "Maybe I can't take care of these horses as well as I thought I could. That's what my boys are saying. They keep telling this old man that he ought to sell the farm and retire."

"But you can't," I gasped.

Mr. Long just smiled. "You're right, Jen," he sighed. "I can't. I always said, if I sell this farm, I might as well pack up and die myself. A man's gotta do what he loves — or a girl, in your case. I've loved horses and this farm here all my life.

But now, well, I'm thinking about lots of things."
Suddenly Mr. Long looked a lot older than he
ever had before. "Can you girls take care of Misty
for a while?" he asked. "I need to make a phone
call or two."

"Sure," we both said together. But something
didn't seem right. It wasn't like Mr. Long to leave
a sick horse to go talk to someone on the phone.

When he was gone, I turned to Keisha. "I think
something's up with Mr. Long."

"He does seem to be acting kind of weird . . . ,"
said Keisha.

"I have a funny feeling it has something to do
with that man you saw here earlier," I told her.
"The guy in the red suv."

"I told you I wasn't making it up!"

"Well, we still don't know what's going on yet,"
I said. "But I think we better try to find out."

CHAPTER 3

We Need a Plan

Keisha and I had to stick to our plan. At our lesson the next day we would ask Mr. Long about the man in the SUV.

We'd try to find out what was really going on. But it turned out we didn't have to ask.

The next day came and Misty was way better but still not good enough for me to ride. I had to ride one of the other horses. That was okay. The new horse could jump almost as well as Misty. Almost. Misty was still my favorite horse.

"That was awesome," said Keisha. I had just finished the last jump of the lesson.

"Great riding, girls," said Mr. Long. "You two are getting to be real good riders, that's for sure." Our lesson was over. It was time to ask about the man in the SUV.

"Mr. Long —," I began. But before I could

finish, the red SUV came into view.

Mr. Long cut me off. "Just a minute, Jen. I gotta talk to this guy." With that, he turned and walked off to the house.

"How come Mr. Sleazebag is back here?" Keisha asked me.

The man with the slicked-back hair had parked his big SUV. Now he was waving at Mr. Long.

"Mr. Long is going to be angry about this," I said.

But to our surprise, Mr. Long waved back. He seemed more than willing to talk to the guy. We were at the other end of the field, just walking the two ponies around. We couldn't hear what they were saying, but they looked like they were getting along just fine.

"What do you think is going on over there?" Keisha asked me.

"I don't know, but I'm going to come up with some way to find out!" I said. I wished I had asked Mr. Long about the guy before this.

Keisha kept walking the ponies. We both felt

like spies, but we couldn't hear a word. After a few minutes, Mr. Long shook the man's hand. Then the man in the suit got back in his car and drove away.

"Let's find out what's going on," said Keisha.

She trotted Frosty over to Mr. Long. Before I could follow, Keisha was shouting. "Hey, Mr. Long, who was that guy?"

As I came up, I could hear Mr. Long say, "That was just Mr. Tyrone."

"What did he want?" I asked. I tried to act like I didn't care too much.

"Oh, he's just another guy who wants to buy the farm. He wants to build houses on all this land." Mr. Long looked over the field. Then he shook his head. "He's willing to give me a lot of dough for it, too."

"But you're not going to sell it, right?" asked Keisha.

"Well, yesterday I shut the door in the guy's face," said Mr. Long. "Today, I kind of listened to what he had to say. You know girls, I'm not getting any younger. After Misty got sick, well, I'm not so sure how long I can keep doing this. I don't want no horses getting sick 'cause I can't take care of 'em."

Keisha looked at me. I gave her a look back. If Mr. Long sold the farm, that would be the end of our riding, period. There wasn't any other stable that would take kids like us who couldn't pay.

Mr. Long seemed to know we were both upset. "Don't worry about it, girls, there are lots of other farms around here that have lessons," he said. And with that he walked away.

As soon as he was gone, Keisha burst out, "We have to do something, Jen! We can't just sit here and see the farm get sold. I mean, this field will get turned into a bunch of houses. And Misty and Frosty . . ."

"Don't even think about it," I told her. "We need a better plan. Can you stay over at my house tonight?" I asked her.

"I guess so. What are we going to do?"

"I think I might have an idea," I told her.

After we put our ponies away, I phoned my mom and asked if Keisha could sleep over. That part was easy. An hour later, my mom drove to Shady Acres to pick us up.

As soon as we got in the car, my mom started talking. I had heard this kind of talk a few hundred times before. "I have no idea why pretty girls like you are hanging around a barn on a nice day like this," she said. "And you know horses are dangerous, girls. . . ."

"Mooommm," I said, rolling my eyes. I didn't feel like hearing a lecture from my mom, and I'm sure Keisha didn't either.

"Well, I just wish you girls were into something a little safer. A lot of girls try ballet or painting," she said.

I tried not to throw up. I could just see myself dancing or painting. It was so . . . not me! So Keisha and I put on our iPods to drown her out.

All the way home, I was busy working out my plan. By the time we pulled into my driveway, I knew what we had to do.

Up in my bedroom I threw myself down on the carpet. Keisha flopped down across from me. "The

problem is that Misty got sick," I told her. "That's why Mr. Long is so upset. If Mr. Long thinks he can't take care of his horses, he'll sell the farm. But if we help him out, if we make it easy for him . . . ," I said, and then I lost my thought.

"Yeah, but we already help him," said Keisha.

"I know," I replied, sitting up. "But what if we *secretly* helped him. That way he'd think he was still doing all the work, but it would be easier?"

Keisha just looked at me. Of the two of us, I was the thinker and she was the doer. I'm the one who comes up with the plans. But Keisha is the one who actually does them. She thinks I'm smart. I think she's gutsy. Friends are like that. We're a lot alike but different too. "So explain," she said.

"So we sneak over early in the morning and do the clean-up. Then Mr. Long thinks the farm isn't so much work, and he won't sell."

Keisha smiled. "That's an awesome idea. That way he won't have to work so hard. And besides, *we* can make sure everything is done right!"

We talked a little longer and decided that we would start the next morning. We'd go extra early to Shady Acres and clean out all the stalls before Mr. Long even got up.

"There's only one problem," said Keisha. "How are we going to get to the barn that early in the morning?"

"Leave that one to me," I said.

That night at dinner I told my parents about a

"special" riding class. I said that Keisha and I had to meet early in the morning, every day, for the rest of the summer. At first my parents didn't like the idea. "I don't know why you have to keep chasing that dream of riding, Jen," my dad said. "It's a waste of time."

"Mr. Long thinks I have a lot of talent," I replied. I knew that would convince my parents. If there's one thing they like, it's me being better at stuff than other kids. "He thinks I could win prizes in jumping or riding."

"Really?" asked my mother.

"Really," I said. It wasn't just a lie. Mr. Long really did think I was a good rider, but I added the prize part. "But I have to practice a lot. And Keisha is going to help me."

Keisha just sat there looking stunned.

"I said, Keisha is going to help me. Aren't you, Keisha?" I said, kicking her with my foot.

"Oh, of course," Keisha told them, joining it. "Jen can always count on me."

I have to admit, Keisha sounded a bit lame.

She's a lousy liar. But in the end, my mom agreed to drive us to the barn at six in the morning.

We only had one simple thing to worry about — we didn't want to get caught by Mr. Long.

CHAPTER 4

Peeking from a Stall

kept dreaming that night. I dreamed about taking Misty over some jumps. Then I dreamed about the man in the red SUV. In the dream, the man was chasing us. I kept telling Misty to go faster, but the man kept getting closer. I woke up when I heard some knocking.

"Jen . . . Keisha." It was my mom, waking us up.

I moaned and rolled over. My clock said 5:30. I saw Keisha open her eyes. She looked at me, still groggy. She was just as tired as I was.

"We're awake, Mom," I croaked. Then I threw off the covers and put my feet on the floor.

Keisha sighed. "Are you sure this is worth it, Jen?" She closed her eyes again.

I grabbed a pillow and whacked her over the head. "Of course it is! Get out of bed, you dork!"

Keisha laughed with me. "Okay, I'm awake. Don't hit me again," she groaned.

Downstairs we both ate some toast and cereal. Keisha was so tired she poured orange juice all over her cereal. "I don't know if I can to do this all summer," she mumbled.

"Yes, you can," I told her. "Just think: if we don't do this, you'll never ride Frosty again. That should wake you up."

"You're right," Keisha said. But her eyes were still half closed.

My mom came into the kitchen. "I don't know about this early morning riding class," she said as she made some coffee. "It seems like it'll be too hard on you girls."

"It's fine, Mom. Mr. Long really thinks we can improve our riding with this class," I said.

"Maybe I should talk to Mr. Long. I don't think little girls should get up this early on summer vacation."

I nearly choked. I could feel Keisha kicking me under the table. If my mom talked to Mr. Long, she would find out there was no class. Then our whole plan would be ruined.

"We're not little, Mom," I told her, still thinking.

"Well, you know what I mean," my mom replied.

"Actually, it's a lot safer for us to ride in the morning," I told her.

"Why's that?" she asked.

"Umm . . ." I was still thinking. "Because it's not so hot in the morning. We won't get heat stroke if we ride in the morning," I said. "Then we won't fall off the horses." I thought my mom would like that since she was always worried about me getting hurt.

"Well it makes sense, I guess," my mom said. "But even still, *I* don't want to be getting up this early every day."

"If you drive us, I promise I'll help out more around the house," I said. My mom *had* to drive us. It would take forever to walk there.

"I'll take your word for it, then," she said grabbing her keys. "Let's go, girls."

When we got to Shady Acres, the barn was dark. "It doesn't look like anyone's here," said my mom.

"We're just a little early," I said, grabbing Keisha by the hand. "Horse people start the day early, Mom," I told her. I didn't want to have to explain anything else. Then I pushed the car door shut.

Luckily, my mom didn't ask us any more questions.

We tiptoed into the barn, trying hard not to make any noise. We were there so early that we even woke up the horses.

Misty began to whinny when she heard us come in.

"Shhh!" I whispered to her. "You'll wake up Mr. Long."

Then Keisha and I went over to her. Keisha petted Misty while I tried to soothe her with my voice. Misty had been nervous ever since she got sick. When a car would come up the drive, she'd begin pacing and snorting. It was as if she was afraid of something. But what was it? *If only Misty could tell us,* I thought.

34

"Where do you want to start?" asked Keisha.

"Why don't we clean out the stalls?" I said.

"But that's the worst job," moaned Keisha.

"Exactly," I agreed. "And it will be the most help to Mr. Long."

So we grabbed some pitchforks and a wheelbarrow. We started at the front of the barn. At each stall, we would take the horse out, tie it up, and then clean up all the poop.

"This is so gross!" said Keisha. "Mr. Long is sure to find out what we're doing. I mean, we're going to stink sooo bad!"

I rolled my eyes.

"I mean, the poop smell is on my hands . . . and in my hair. I think it's even soaked into my eyes!"

"Keisha, shhh!" I told her.

We were just moving to the next stall when we heard footsteps on the gravel outside. We froze. I looked at Keisha. She looked back at me with wide eyes.

Even Misty was upset. She must have known something was wrong. She began breathing hard and pounding her hooves on the stall door.

Is Misty trying to warn us, I thought.

"Mr. Long doesn't come out to the barn this early," Keisha whispered.

"We've got to hide!" I whispered back. Slowly we rolled the wheelbarrow into a corner. Then we pulled the horse back into his stall. When I saw the barn door open, I grabbed Keisha and shut us into an empty stall.

We were both breathing hard. I was afraid that Mr. Long would hear us, but he didn't seem to. After a few minutes Keisha and I poked our heads above the stall door and peeked out into the barn.

We both gasped. It wasn't Mr. Long in the barn, it was Mr. Tyrone! It was the guy with the suv!

Mr. Tyrone was looking around for something. He looked creepy, sneaking around the barn. A few more minutes went by. At last, Mr. Tyrone seemed to have found what he was looking for. He stopped at the barrel of oats and took a bottle out of his pocket.

He looked around to make sure there was no

one else in the barn. He waited. Then he poured
the stuff from the bottle into the oats.

I couldn't believe what he was doing. I was
about to march out there and confront him.
That's when Keisha grabbed my hand. "Don't,"
she whispered. I think she had read my mind.

I sighed. Keisha was right, I couldn't confront
him. Who knew what he might do to me and

Keisha. Besides, we had no excuse to be in the barn. We had no more right to be here than he did.

So we both stayed in our hiding spots. When Mr. Tyrone left the barn, Keisha and I let out sighs of relief. We hadn't been caught. We hadn't got in trouble. But now there were a whole bunch of other problems we had to solve.

CHAPTER 5

Ready to Get in Trouble?

"**N**ow it all makes sense!" I said to Keisha. "Mr. Tyrone must have put poison in Misty's feed. He's trying to scare Mr. Long off the farm!"

"So what are we going to do?" asked Keisha. "We can't let Mr. Long know we were here — he'll be super mad at us!"

Keisha had a point. How could we let Mr. Long know about the oats without getting ourselves in trouble? But if we didn't tell him, he'd just feed the oats to the horses. Then all of them would get sick, not just Misty.

"Are you ready to get in trouble?" I asked Keisha.

"You want us to tell Mr. Long?" she asked.

"If it means saving all the horses from getting sick, yeah. I'll risk it," I said.

"We'll be toast," Keisha said.

"Toast it is," I told her. I gritted my teeth.

We kept on cleaning the stalls. When Mr. Long came down to the barn, we had at least helped him out a little. Maybe that would save us from getting into too much trouble.

About an hour later, around 7:30, we heard Mr. Long whistling and walking toward the barn. By this time all the horses were awake. Some of them were neighing, waiting for breakfast.

When he opened the barn door, Keisha and I were standing in the middle of the aisle. We didn't even try to hide. Of course, Mr. Long was really surprised to see us. He smiled at first, but then his smile turned into a frown. "I thought I told you girls that no one is allowed down here if I'm not around," he said. "It's not safe."

"Don't be mad," I said, trying to look as sweet as I could.

"We do have something to tell you!" Keisha blurted out. "It's about Mr. Tyrone."

Mr. Long shot a look at both of us. "At the crack of dawn, you're going to tell me a story?" he asked.

"Yes," I replied. "Please, just listen."

So Mr. Long listened to our whole story. At the end, it was simple. "I think he fed Misty the same stuff he put in the oats!" I said. "That's what made Misty sick."

Mr. Long just looked at us for a long time, not saying anything.

"Well, girls, I don't know if I should be mad or glad right now," he began.

"Don't be mad Mr. Long," Keisha replied. "We were only trying to help. And look, we *did* clean out all the stalls."

That seemed to make Mr. Long a little happier. "Okay, girls, I'll let you off this time. And I gotta

41

thank you for cleanin' up the barn. But I mean it — you can't come down here when I'm not around," he said. He looked very stern.

"We won't," we both said.

"Now I don't know what to make of this here story of yours. Poison in the oats, you say. Tyrone sneaking around here. Well, I can't hardly believe it."

"But it's true," I told him. "We saw him!"

"Yeah, and once I saw a chicken play piano. But

I'm willing to check it out. If there's something in these oats, we got a big problem. If there's nothin', then you girls have got a big problem. You hear me?"

"Yes, sir," Keisha said. I don't think she'd ever called Mr. Long "sir" before.

"I'm going to take them oats off to the vet," said Mr. Long, "We'll have 'em tested and find out what's what. While I'm doing that, can you girls put a scoop of the fresh oats in each feed bucket?"

"Yes, sir," we said.

In no time, Mr. Long was back with a big sack of fresh oats. He used a can to scoop out some of the poisoned oats. Then Mr. Long headed off to the vet's office. He told us not to ride any of the horses while he was gone.

So all we could do was wait. We cleaned some of the saddles and picked a few rocks out of the riding ring. By lunch time, we were dead beat. It's tough getting up at 5:30 and working all morning.

Then Mr. Long's truck came racing up the driveway. The way he was driving, I could tell he was mad. He stopped right by us and hopped out of the truck, still holding the can of oats.

"Well, girls, you were right. Looks like Mr. Tyrone really wants me out of here," he said. "He wants this place so bad he's even ready to poison my horses!"

Even though I was upset, I can't say I was surprised. After all, Keisha and I saw the guy dumping the stuff into the oats. If his plan had worked, Mr. Long might never have known why his horses got sick. But we figured it out.

"So what are you going to do?" Keisha asked Mr. Long.

"I guess I'll have myself a stake-out tonight," Mr. Long told us. "I'll catch the guy red-handed."

Keisha and I looked at each other. We were both thinking the same thing. "Can we help?" we both asked together.

"I don't think so, girls. It's too darn risky," said Mr. Long. "Any guy that would poison a horse ain't going to be too nice to you or me. Besides, I don't think your parents would allow it."

44

"But we wouldn't tell them!" I said. Right away I realized how dumb that was.

"I'm not going to have you girls doing anything your parents don't know about," he said. "How'd you get out here so early, anyway?"

"My mom drove us," I told him. But that's all I said. I didn't tell Mr. Long about the phony riding lesson.

So we finally got to ride our horses that day. I took Misty around the far field with Keisha riding Frosty right beside me. Misty still wasn't ready to take jumps, but she was trotting just like always. In another couple of days, she'd be just fine.

While we were riding, I got a brainwave. "I have an idea," I shouted to Keisha

"Uh-oh," she said. Even before I told her, she knew what I had in mind. My idea meant breaking the rules again. But what choice did we have?

CHAPTER 6

By Moonlight

It was just before midnight. I was dressed all in black as I snuck out the back door of my house. I closed the door as softly as I could. I just hoped that my parents didn't hear. If they knew what I was doing, they would kill me.

The plan was simple. Keisha and I would sneak out of our houses. Then we'd hike over to Shady Acres and try to help Mr. Long.

"Mr. Long is real old. What if Mr. Tyrone does something to him?" Keisha had said. I think she

was scared by my idea.

"We'll bring your mom's cell phone," I told her. "We can call the police if something bad happens."

Keisha rolled her eyes at me. She didn't like this, any of it. But she went along. A good friend will always go along with you — even if it's kind of crazy.

It was only a short walk over to Keisha's house.

The plan was to meet there and then hike to Shady Acres.

When I got to Keisha's house, I tapped on her bedroom window. A few seconds later she opened it. "I thought you'd never get here," she whispered. Then she climbed out the window and jumped onto the ground.

Keisha was dressed all in black, too. She had brought two flashlights. "I thought we might need these," she said. "After all, there aren't any streetlights out in the country."

I guess I hadn't thought of that. The walk to Mr. Long's farm would take a good hour and it was down a winding dirt road. It was the kind of road you see in horror movies. I could just imagine something hiding in the trees.

Even though Keisha was brave when we left town, I could tell she was starting to get spooked in the country. It looks different at night. There were trees all around us and I kept hearing twigs snap, like there was someone — or something — out there.

"Maybe this isn't such a good idea," Keisha said.

We had been walking pretty much in silence up until then.

"Don't be a baby," I snapped at her. Then we walked on in the darkness.

At long last, we saw the Shady Acres sign. We both let out a sigh of relief. It was still pitch dark, but somehow it felt safer now that we had reached the farm.

We knew that Mr. Long planned on waiting inside the barn. My plan was to wait outside. That way we'd be able to stay out of Mr. Long's sight. And we'd be the first to know if Mr. Tyrone was coming.

We sat on a bale of hay at one side of the barn. From there, we could see the barn door and up to the house. Then all we could do was wait.

"It's kind of creepy out here," Keisha whispered.

"I know," I whispered back. I sure wished we could talk more. It would've made me forget about the bugs and the weird howling of the wind.

We must have been waiting an hour when Keisha spoke again. I guess I must have been asleep, because her whisper made me jump.

"Maybe we should just go home," she whispered. "I don't think the guy is going to show up tonight. Plus, I don't know how much more of this creepiness I can take."

"Ri-ight," I groaned. "It's not even three o'clock . . . and you want to give up."

"I'm not saying give up, but . . . "

Keisha didn't finish. Just then, I heard footsteps. I grabbed Keisha's arm, and I knew that she heard the footsteps too.

In the moonlight, I could see Mr. Tyrone opening the barn door. When he made it inside, I grabbed Keisha's hand.

"Okay, call the police," I whispered.

She pushed the green "on" button on the cell phone and we waited. And waited.

"Maybe it's not charged up," Keisha whispered.

"You didn't check?" I was ready to scream.

"Well, I just thought . . ."

Then we both heard Mr. Long's voice, "What do you think you're doing, Tyrone?" The lights in the barn flicked on.

"Quick," I whispered to Keisha. "Over to the window."

There were some shuffling and grunting sounds inside the barn. I looked at Keisha. We both knew we had to do something. But then we heard Mr. Long's voice again.

"Okay, okay, I give up," he gasped. "Just get off me!"

CHAPTER 7

Who Gives Up?

Keisha and I crawled over to the barn window. Then the two of us peeked inside.

There was Mr. Long, lying on the floor. On top of him was Mr. Tyrone, holding him down.

"You won't get the farm like this," Mr. Long said.

"You're a fool," said Mr. Tyrone. He got off the old man's chest and began pacing. "I offered you good money. You could just take the money and go live anyplace. You could go retire. Go take it easy. Forget these stupid horses."

"Not while I'm still alive and kicking," Mr. Long told him. He sat up on the floor. I could see some blood dripping beside his mouth.

"That may not be long, old man," Mr. Tyrone told him. "Your boys will sell to me after you're gone. The only problem is *you*. You're just too stubborn for your own good."

"So what are you going to do to me, Tyrone?" Mr. Long spat at him. "Kill me?"

Mr. Tyrone just smiled, a really sick smile. "Not me, old man. I wouldn't do something like that. But sometimes accidents happen." He looked around the barn. "In an old place like this, lots of accidents might happen."

That's all I needed to hear. I turned to Keisha and said, "Let's roll."

Keisha gave me a look of panic, but there was no choice. I pulled open the barn door and raced inside.

Mr. Long and Mr. Tyrone both looked up.

"Jen . . . what . . . ?" Mr. Long asked. He smiled when he saw me.

"What are you doing up so late, girl?" Mr. Tyrone asked. He had a sick smile on his face, as if there was nothing wrong.

But I knew better. "We heard it all," I told him. My heart was beating so fast I thought it would explode. "We're going to tell the police what you said."

"Who's the 'we,' kid?" Mr. Tyrone shot back. "Looks to me like there's just the three of us."

That's when I looked around. *Where was Keisha? Where was my friend?*

Mr. Tyrone slowly began moving toward me. I backed away, scared. I wondered if I should run. I wondered if I could get to help in time. But where was Keisha? Why wasn't my friend here to help us?

At last, Mr. Tyrone backed me up against the wall. I looked around for something, anything. Then I saw the pitchfork. I grabbed it.

"I'll use this," I told him, holding put the pitchfork. "I'll . . . I'll. . . ."

He was too fast for me. In no time, he kicked the pitchfork out of my hands. Then he reached out to grab me.

He would have had me, too, but there was a sound. One of the horses snorted and whinnied. Mr. Tyrone turned to look. Then there was a smash as a stall door flew open.

It was Misty! She was coming right at Mr. Tyrone and me. Riding on her, bareback, was Keisha. And Keisha was holding a shovel.

"Let's get him, Misty," Keisha shouted. She lifted the shovel and galloped toward us.

When Mr. Tyrone saw Misty coming, he fell to the floor. He covered his head with his hands, ready for the worst.

Misty slammed to a stop right in front of him. Keisha held the shovel, ready to hit Mr. Tyrone if he dared to get up.

But Mr. Tyrone was scared to death. He stayed down on the floor, almost crying.

"Get that animal away from me! I give . . .
I give!"

CHAPTER 8

You Could Have Been Killed

The next little while was just a blur for all of us. Mr. Long got off the floor and picked up the pitchfork. He and Misty made sure that Mr. Tyrone stayed trapped on the floor. I ran off to the house and dialed 911.

Pretty soon the Shady Acres farm was full of people. There were two police cars, plus a few reporters who must've heard about it somehow. I guess Mr. Tyrone was quite a big shot around town. His getting arrested was big news.

The police took down what we said. I guess the whole thing was pretty clear. Of course, we'd have to talk to the police again in the morning. But as soon as Mr. Tyrone was in handcuffs, Keisha and I gave each other a high five. We were so happy that we didn't notice Mr. Long standing there. He had his hands on his hips, staring at us.

"Jen," said Keisha.

"What?" I said, looking at her.

"Um, I think Mr. Long wants to talk to us."

I could see that Mr. Long was pretty upset. He should have been happy, but there was no smile on his face as he paced back and forth.

"I've called your parents," he began.

I let out a gasp. Both Keisha and I knew that we were in major trouble now. We had both snuck out of our houses. My parents would ground me for a month, or maybe for life.

"They're going to find out anyway," Mr. Long said. "Better if we explain it tonight. If they read it in the papers, you'll be in big trouble."

Just then I saw Keisha's parents' car pull into

the driveway. My parents' car came roaring in after that. As soon as both cars stopped, the bunch of them stormed toward us.

"Here goes," I said looking at Keisha.

Misty began whinnying when she heard the car door slam. Maybe she knew that it was our parents. And maybe she knew how much trouble we'd be in.

My mom came rushing in first, shooting nasty looks at all of us. "Jen, you could have been killed," my mom began. She seemed happy that I wasn't but still mad as anything.

Keisha's mom came second. She was angry, too. "Keisha," said her mom, "how many times . . ."

"Young lady, you are in so much trouble . . ." said Keisha's dad.

"I can't believe this," my dad joined in. "I don't care if these riding lessons *are* free, you're never coming out here again."

I'd never seen my dad this mad. And it wasn't fair. I mean, we were heroes. We'd saved Mr. Long's life. And now this!

It was Mr. Long who went to bat for us.

"Now, wait a minute here," Mr. Long broke in. "Go easy on these two girls. They saved my bacon tonight."

"But they could have been killed!" my mom shouted.

"But they weren't," Mr. Long said. "And they're safe, now. That's the important thing. These two girls really stuck their necks out to save this old man and this farm. You try to stop them from coming out here, and you're just nuts."

We looked at our parents. They seemed to be calming down.

Mr. Long went on. "You should be proud of these girls. They're smart and gutsy and ready to fight for what they want. Jen and Keisha deserve a medal or two, not you folks shouting at them. What kind of parents are you, anyhow?"

Suddenly it was quiet. I think my parents felt bad. They had been wrong, and they knew it.

"But you did sneak out without telling me," said Keisha's mom. "So don't think you're getting off scott-free. You'll have to. . . ." She stopped to think.

"Wash dishes all summer?" Keisha suggested.

"Right," said her mom. "And help Mr. Long with his horses."

Out of the corner of my eye I could see Keisha grinning. The dishes were nothing at all. Helping out Mr. Long was what we wanted to do all summer anyway.

I looked at my parents.

But they took their cue from Keisha's mom. "The same goes for you, Jen," said my mom. "And if you ever sneak out again. . . ."

"I'll be toast."

"Worse than toast," my mom added. "You'll be a burnt crust of bread, grounded for life."

"But in the meanwhile?" I asked.

"In the meanwhile, I guess you can keep on riding."

ALSO BY LIZ BROWN

The Bully

by LIZ BROWN

Sugar and spice and everything . . . mean. Allison finds that the worst bully at her school is a girl, and the worst weapon can be a whisper.

Dark Ryder

by LIZ BROWN

Kate Hanson finally gets the horse of her dreams, but Dark Ryder comes with a catch. Kate has just three months to turn him into a winner, or she'll lose her horse forever.

OTHER HIP TITLES YOU MIGHT ENJOY

The Crash

by PAUL KROPP

A school bus slides off a cliff in a snowstorm. The bus driver is out cold. One of the guys is badly hurt. Can Craig, Rory and Lerch find help in time?

Three Feet Under

by PAUL KROPP

Scott and Rico find a map to long-lost treasure. There's $250,000 buried in Bolton's mine. But when the school bully steals their map and heads for the old mine, the race is on.

Bats Past Midnight

by SHARON JENNINGS
Sam and Simon wonder about a fancy car that hangs around their school late at night. When they try to find out more, they end up in trouble at school, at home and with the police.

Bats in the Graveyard

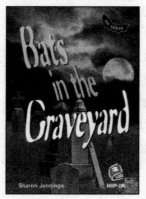

by SHARON JENNINGS
Sam and Simon have to look after Simon's little sister on Halloween night. Soon the boys end up in a cemetery — spooked!

Pump

by SHARON JENNINGS

A young 'boarder and his friends try to get their town to build a skateboarding park. But Pat finds the town meeting a lot scarier than any half-pipe.

My Broken Family

by PAUL KROPP

Divorce is always rotten. When Maddy's parents split up, her whole life starts to fall apart. But when it's all over, she finds that love is stronger than she thought.

ABOUT THE AUTHOR

Liz Brown has loved horses ever since she was a little girl, long before she went to Ryerson University to study journalism. She was lucky enough to grow up on a horse farm with two ponies, Misty and Frosty. Unlike the girls in *Misty Knows*, Liz never had to solve a mystery at the stables where she learned to ride. Liz now divides her time between magazine journalism and teaching kids how to ride. She has written *Dark Ryder,* another novel about horses, and *The Bully* for HIP Sr.

For more information on the books we publish, contact:

High Interest Publishing – Publishers of H•I•P Books

www.hip-books.com | 1-877-562-6602 | hip-books@sympatico.ca